Items should be returned on or before the last date shown below. Items not already requested by other borrowers may be renewed in person, in writing or by telephone. To renew, please quote the number on the barcode label. To renew online a PIN is required. This can be requested at your local library.
Renew online @ **www.dublincitypubliclibraries.ie**
Fines charged for overdue items will include postage incurred in recovery. Damage to or loss of items will be charged to the borrower.

Leabharlanna Poiblí Chathair Bhaile Átha Cliath
Dublin City Public Libraries

Baile Átha Cliath
Dublin City

Brainse Mheal Ráthluirc
Charleville Mall Branch
Tel. 8749619

1 MAR 2017

Date Due	Date Due	Date Due

The radio crackled on the kitchen table...

"In 1848, on the quay of New Ross in County Wexford, President John F. Kennedy's great-grandfather, Patrick Kennedy, boarded a famine ship and made the long journey to America. And now, 115 years later, the White House has confirmed that President Kennedy will return to his ancestral home, New Ross, as part of his extended trip to Ireland..."

"He wasn't president when he was here...
That's the way he wanted to be, I think.
He wanted to be just one of ourselves."
— Josie Grennan, the Kennedys' cousin

For Ella and Julia, they haven't invented that word yet and you know why — x x.

And for Christopher, Sean-Felipe, Santiago and Katie, the next generation of Tubridys — keep it goofy.

Enormous gratitude to Deirdre and Maria at Walker Books who warmly and kindly and with great humour cajoled me hither and thither to breathe life into Patrick and his world.

Also, thank you to P.J. for giving me the privilege of having his beautiful art associated with my simple story.

❖ R.T.

For Ronan, Teresa, Rory, Oscar and Flora.

With thanks to my models, particularly Paddy, Dermot and Saibh. Thanks also to Sam, Ben, Evie, Barbara, Julia and Ryan.

I also want to acknowledge the generous help I received from Patrick Grennan of the Kennedy Homestead Visitor Centre, Dunganstown, County Wexford, and Sam Rubin of the John F. Kennedy Presidential Library and Museum in Boston.

❖ P.J.L.

Song lyrics to "The Boys of Wexford" reproduced with kind permission from the President's Office Files,
John F. Kennedy Presidential Library and Museum.

Painting of The Irish Times newspaper included with thanks to The Irish Times.

First published 2017 by Walker Books Ltd, 87 Vauxhall Walk, London SE11 5HJ ❖ Text © 2017 Ryan Tubridy ❖ Illustrations © 2017 P. J. Lynch ❖ The right of Ryan Tubridy and P. J. Lynch to be identified as author and illustrator respectively of this work has been asserted by them in accordance with the Copyright, Designs and Patents Act 1988 ❖ This book has been typeset in Bodoni Egyptian Pro Medium ❖ Printed in China ❖ All rights reserved. No part of this book may be reproduced, transmitted or stored in an information retrieval system in any form or by any means, graphic, electronic or mechanical, including photocopying, taping and recording, without prior written permission from the publisher. ❖ British Library Cataloguing in Publication Data:a catalogue record for this book is available from the British Library ❖ ISBN 978-1-4063-6692-1 ❖ www.walker.co.uk ❖ 10 9 8 7 6 5 4 3 2 1

PATRICK
AND THE
PRESIDENT

RYAN TUBRIDY
P. J. LYNCH

WALKER BOOKS
AND SUBSIDIARIES
LONDON · BOSTON · SYDNEY · AUCKLAND

Patrick had been trying to teach his dog, Bing, to sit when
the news was broadcast – the 35th president of the United States
of America was coming to Wexford, to Patrick's very own home town.

Patrick's daddy began leaping around the room with delight,
his mammy was near-giddy with excitement, and Bing was
definitely in no mood to stay still – now he was up on his hind legs,
dancing round the kitchen.

"Well, that's settled so!" Patrick's daddy said. "'Himself' is coming.
There'll be some commotion that week. Can you imagine what this
will do to the town?"

"Oh, I just knew he'd come," said Patrick's mammy with a sigh,
looking dreamily off into the distance. "Sure, his people are from here,
so why wouldn't he? I'm only dying to see him. He's like something
from the movies!"

At school that Monday, there was only one topic in the yard – the president's visit to Ireland.

"His helicopter is the size of a spaceship," proclaimed Victor Delaney, who had every intention of visiting the moon by his twelfth birthday.

Carmel Minihan told anyone who would listen that she knew *for a fact* that the president's car was as long as two houses.

"The windows are *this* thick," she said, her arms stretched out as far as they could go. Even shy John Synott got in his tuppence worth: Secret Servicemen wore X-ray specs.

"True story!" he said with a flourish.

It was normally cold in Patrick's school, even in April, but that morning at assembly the air was hot – humming with anticipation. The children knew something was up.

Standing at the top of the hall, Father Power signalled for calm and quiet, getting both much quicker than usual. With a quick cough to clear his throat, he addressed his young audience.

"As you well know, boys and girls, President Kennedy is coming to Ireland. More precisely, he is coming home – his family was from New Ross. When the president lands on O'Kennedy Park, he will be greeted by a choir of schoolchildren…" He paused. "And *you*, boys and girls…" Father Power paused again and beamed. *"You* will be the choir!"

The hall erupted into an enormous chorus of cheers,
the children's eyes and smiles wide and bright.

When the first flurry of excitement died down,
Patrick raised his hand.
"Excuse me Father, is this … true?
Will we really be there? All of us? Singing?
For the president of the United States?"
Five questions in one breath, a new record for Patrick.

But Father Power didn't mind.
"Yes, Patrick," he said, "each and every one of you."

A new burst of frenzied chitter-chatter filled the hall.
The president! What will we sing, do you think?
Will we have to wear uniforms?
What will he be like?

Patrick couldn't wait to get home.

He raced through the door to his mammy – almost tripping over an excitable Bing, hot on his heels – and fourteen different things tumbled out of his mouth all at once.

"A-a-a-and … I might actually get to *meet* the president!" Patrick finally said to her, breathless and flushed. His mammy gently pressed a cool hand to his cheek and, bursting at the seams with pride, scooped Patrick up into her arms.

By the time Patrick's daddy came home from his job at the Ritz Cinema, the whole house was abuzz with Kennedy chat. Thanks to the newsreels they showed before each film, Patrick's daddy knew everything there was to know about it.

"You'll never guess who I bumped into today!" said Patrick's daddy.
"Only President Kennedy's nearest relatives in Ireland – the Ryan girls!
So it seems the Ryans are hosting a big tea party at the homestead in
Dunganstown, and they'll be serving cake and sandwiches to the
president and his sisters…"

Patrick's daddy paused dramatically.
His wife gave him a friendly shove. "Oh now, come on, out with it!
This isn't a movie you're in now!"

"Well," he replied with a grin, "I offered up young Patrick's
services to help at the tea party."

Patrick opened his mouth. Closed it. Opened it.
"You look like a little goldfish!" his daddy said with a laugh.
"I take it you're available, then?"

For the next three weeks, Patrick stayed back after school with all the other boys and girls, practising and perfecting the three songs they would perform. Lying in bed at night, staring up at his ceiling, Patrick would mumble the words: *"We are the Boys of Wexford, who fought with heart and hand..."*

And in the morning, when he woke, the lyrics were already in his mouth: *"In comes the captain's daughter, the captain of the Yeos, saying, 'Brave United Irishmen, we'll ne'er again be foes.'"*

At the weekend, Patrick went to the Ryans' to rehearse his Swiss roll responsibilities:

- Take one raspberry Swiss roll.
- Slice it into six equal parts.
- Place it – "Easy now. A bit more gently than that, good lad!"
  – neatly onto a fine china plate.

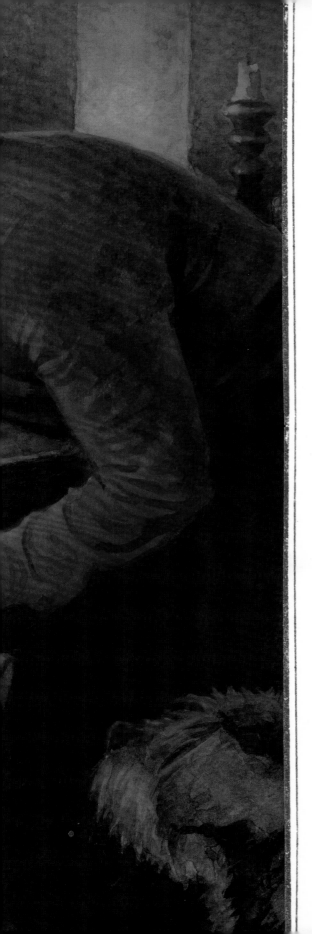

At last, at 8.03 p.m. on 26 June, the president landed in Ireland.

Patrick and his parents huddled around the radio and listened to President de Valera welcome Ireland's most famous returning emigrant, describing him as "a distinguished scion of our race, who has won first place amongst his fellow countrymen, first in a nation of one hundred and eighty million people".

Patrick looked at his father. "Did he say one hundred and eighty million? Are there really one hundred and eighty *million* people in America?"

"Yes, son," replied his daddy. "Now, listen closely. It doesn't get much better than this for one of our own."

A day later, on the morning of the president's visit to New Ross, Patrick woke at 6 a.m. It felt like Christmas; he'd barely managed twenty minutes' sleep.

Patrick was never so careful getting dressed.

He kept a very giddy Bing at arm's length while his mother made the final checks: she smoothed his cowlick, polished the dried mud off his left shoe, then licked a tissue and dabbed at his face.

And, with one final *"RightbyeseeyoulateryeahIknowIknow!"*, Patrick was hurtling out the door, heading for O'Kennedy Park.

At O'Kennedy Park, everyone's gaze was firmly fixed on the sky.

Waiting.

Suddenly, the silence was shattered. Carmel Minihan let out a yelp and gestured wildly to the sky. "There it is! He's coming!"

Sure enough, a roar and a *hummmmm-brummm* filled the sky, and soon after, an enormous green metal bird slowly descended towards the field. Within seconds of the motor stopping, business-like men with cameras around their necks and notebooks in their hands emerged.

"They're the journalists," whispered Victor Delaney, knowingly.

When a second helicopter landed, another lot of men emptied out, but this time in tan coats and jet-black sunglasses.

"You see, didn't I tell ye?" John Synott exclaimed to no one in particular, unable to take his eyes off the men.

But, still ... no sign of the president.

Five long minutes later, the air felt like it was vibrating and a rumble ripped through the clouds. As the whirring blades slowed, the door opened, and the steps came down. Patrick stood on his tippy-toes and squinted to focus until he finally saw…

Himself.

The president of the United States.

The children had just burst into "The Boys of Wexford" when Carmel started nudging Patrick in the back. The president was approaching.

The children suddenly sang louder – reaching deeper and deeper for every note. As they neared the end of the song, Patrick could just about see the president, standing at Father Power's shoulder; he wanted to join in for a verse! Soon, the children's voices were intermingled with the deep baritone of President Kennedy, who grinned his way through the tune, patting freshly shampooed heads and shaking little outstretched hands.

Patrick reached up – they all did – wanting so desperately to know what it would feel like to shake the president's hand…

Outside, Patrick could see the Sunday-best clad legs
and elbows of those clamouring to meet Himself.
He tried to make his way through the crowds but there
was no clear path. Suddenly, his chest began to feel tight …
he only had this one chance.

"Over here, Patrick!" a voice called out.
Patrick turned and there was his daddy, arms
outstretched, grinning. "This way, son!"

Patrick protected his plate of cake and, with his daddy
steering his elbow, they dipped and dodged their way
to the front of the pack, finally emerging out into the yard.

Patrick breathed a huge sigh of relief before looking up…

Time slowed down as Patrick's eyes met those of President Kennedy. As if in a dream, Patrick raised his hand...

JFK took it. And shook it.

"Is that for me?" the president asked, smiling and nodding towards the Swiss roll. Patrick looked at his plate, looked back up at Himself and offered up his perfectly sliced Swiss roll. The tanned hand reached out and picked up a slice.

"Well, that is just delicious. Thank you, young man."

Patrick was soon swallowed up by the crowd.

His legs felt like jelly, his head dizzy.

His parents found him soon enough, and Bing too,
of course.

"Don't ever wash that lucky hand of yours!"
said Patrick's mammy, hugging him to her,
and his daddy roared laughing.

They told the story of Patrick and the president
many times that day ...
   and the next ...
      and for a long, long time to come.

THE STORY OF PRESIDENT JOHN F. KENNEDY'S VISIT TO IRELAND IN 1963

In 1960, forty-three-year-old John Fitzgerald Kennedy was elected president of the United States – the youngest person and the first ever Catholic to hold that office. On 22 November, 1963, JFK was assassinated in Dallas, Texas. The death of this charismatic and energetic world leader was mourned the world over, and to this day he is considered one of the best-loved figures in American history.

John F. Kennedy always had close personal ties to Ireland. In the late 1840s, during the devastating potato famine, all eight of his great-grandparents left Ireland and immigrated to Boston, Massachusetts, where several family members became successful politicians. JFK treasured his Irish heritage, and after his presidential inauguration he was determined to return to his ancestral home and walk once more in the footsteps of his forefathers.

In April 1963, it was announced in Ireland that the American president was coming to visit. His trip was planned with military precision, and at every stop along his four-day trip tens of thousands of people flocked to catch a glimpse of him. For a whole generation of Irish people, JFK's visit to Ireland became a momentous and unforgettable occasion in their lives.

"This is not the land of my birth, but it is the land for which I hold the greatest affection." – John F. Kennedy

Credit: John Dominis/The LIFE Picture Collection/Getty Images

The motorcade of President John F. Kennedy makes its way down crowd-lined O'Connell Street during his visit to Dublin.

26 JUNE 1963 – DAY ONE

Dublin

At 8 p.m., Air Force One touches down at Dublin Airport. JFK is greeted by President Éamon de Valera and Taoiseach Prime Minister Seán Lemass. The Irish and American presidents both make short, formal speeches. With a twenty-five man motorcycle escort, they then make their way to Áras an Uachtaráin in Phoenix Park, the residence of the Irish president. As the motorcade passes through the city centre, more than 60,000 people line O'Connell Street to catch a glimpse of Kennedy.

27 JUNE 1963 – DAY TWO

New Ross

JFK travels by helicopter to O'Kennedy Park in New Ross, County Wexford. From the air, he sees the word FÁILTE (WELCOME) spelled out by the shapes of children from the local school. A smiling and waving Kennedy is greeted by the Artane Boys' Band, and a choir of 300 schoolchildren sing "The Boys of Wexford", known to be a favourite of the president's. The president walks over and joins in on the second chorus, causing one American photographer to burst into tears. Afterwards, President Kennedy shakes hands with as many schoolchildren as he can reach. Later, addressing the crowds at the quays in New Ross, JFK says, "I am glad to be here. It took 115 years to make this trip. And 6,000 miles. And three generations. And I am proud to be here."

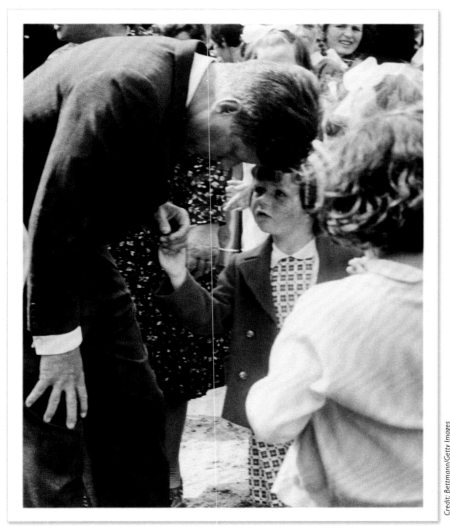

John F. Kennedy interacts with a child in the crowd while he visits his family's ancestral home in Dunganstown.

Credit: Bettmann/Getty Images

Dunganstown

JFK is driven to the Kennedy family homestead in Dunganstown, County Wexford. He is greeted by his distant cousin Mary Ryan and meets many more members of the extended Ryan and Kennedy families. After visiting his cousins, JFK admires the feast that has been prepared for him outside: scones, Swiss rolls, sandwiches and tea. There is even a large cake with his image on the icing. Kennedy remarks, "We want to drink a cup of tea to all the Kennedys who went and all the Kennedys who stayed."

Wexford Harbour

At the Wexford harbourside, Kennedy lays a wreath in memory of Wexford-born commodore John Barry, America's first commissioned naval officer, and is presented with the Freedom of the Town of Wexford.

Dublin: Iveagh House

Kennedy attends a state dinner and reception at the Department of External Affairs, Iveagh House, St Stephen's Green, in his honour.

28 JUNE 1963 – DAY THREE

Cork

Kennedy travels to Cork by helicopter and attends a reception in his honour.

Dublin: Arbour Hill

Kennedy returns to Dublin and visits Arbour Hill Cemetery, where he places a wreath on the graves of the executed leaders of the 1916 Easter Rising, becoming the first foreign head of state to honour them in a formal ceremony.

Leinster House

Kennedy addresses a Joint Sitting of the Houses of the Oireachtas (legislature) in Leinster House. A huge crowd gathers outside, awaiting a glimpse of the president.

Dublin Castle

Kennedy makes his way to St Patrick's Hall in Dublin Castle, where he receives honorary degrees from both the National University of Ireland and Dublin University.

29 JUNE 1963 – DAY FOUR

Galway

On his visit to Galway, Kennedy tells the gathered crowd, "If the day was clear enough, and if you went down to the bay and you looked west, and your sight was good enough, you would see Boston, Massachusetts."

Limerick

Kennedy greets crowds at Greenpark Racecourse in Limerick.

Shannon

Before his departure from Shannon Airport, Kennedy is heard to remark, "I wish I could stay here for another week, or another month."

Credit: Aubrey Hart/Stringer/Hulton Archive/Getty Images

John F. Kennedy is served tea and cake by his distant cousin Mary Ryan at his Dunganstown homestead.